Contents

ta-da

Pedigree®

HiT entertainment

Published 2011.
Pedigree Books Ltd, Beech Hill House,
Walnut Gardens, Exeter, Devon EX4 4DH
books@pedigreegroup.co.uk I www.pedigreebooks.com

£7.99

Hello,

I'm Angelina Ballerina, and I love dancing more than anything in the world. I'm guessing you do too. You're going to have so much fun with this amazing Annual.

It's packed full of great things to make and do and you can read all about my latest adventures in four fantastic stories.

It's a super-exciting time for me. I've moved to the other side of Chipping Cheddar and I've started at a new school called Camembert Academy, where I've met some wonderful new mouseling friends.

Why not start off by flicking through my Fabulous Friendship Files to find out all about the special people in my life?

Happy reading and remember, the world is your stage!

Lots of love,

Angelina

everything Angelina

Name: Angelina Ballerina

Favourite colour: Pink

Dancing dream: To be the best prima ballerina in the whole world.

Favourite dance move: The *grand jeté*, of course!

Best way to spend a Saturday: Eating scones; putting on a show for Mum and Dad with my best friend Alice.

I say, I say: 'I promise to put my best toe forward.'

· ·

PSSST! DID YOU KNOW?
I've got my very own dance studio in the attic! Why don't you come over and practise with me some time?

I'm a dancing princess.

Angelina in a nutshell
Energetic / Determined / Imaginative

all about Alice

Name: Alice Nimbletoes

Favourite colour: Green

Dancing dream: To be a world-class gymnast – though I still love ballet.

Favourite dance move: The *pas de deux* – especially with Angelina as my partner.

Best way to spend a Saturday: Ice-skating or going to Angelina's for muffins – her mum makes the best cakes in Mouseland.

I say, I say: 'This is the best fun ever.'

PSSST! DID YOU KNOW?
I can do a handstand, a walkover and a backflip. Can you?

Alice in a nutshell
Optimistic / Adventurous /
Mischievous

Step it up.

Angelina's Fabulous Friendship Files:

you and your bff

Alice and I are BFFs (that's best friends forever). We love spending time playing, chatting and dancing together. Do you have a BFF? Yes? Well, why don't you fill in these friendship file sections for yourself and for your best friend too?

My Name: ....

Favourite colour: ....

Dancing dream: ....

Favourite dance move: ....

Best way to spend a Saturday: ....

....

....

I say, I say: ....

....

PSSST! DID YOU KNOW?

....

....

BFF Name: ....

Favourite colour: ....

Dancing dream: ....

Favourite dance move: ....

Best way to spend a Saturday: ....

....

....

I say, I say: ....

....

PSSST! DID YOU KNOW?

Stick a photo of yourself here.

Stick a photo of your BFF here.

Me in a nutshell

My BFF in a nutshell

Viki
revealed

Name: Viki

Favourite colour: Citrus shades like tangerine and lemon

Dancing dream: To try out every dance style – I love everything from salsa to street dance.

Favourite dance move: The *pirouette*

Best way to spend a Saturday: learning new moves at a flamenco workshop.

I say, I say: 'This is sooooooo amazing.'

PSSST! DID YOU KNOW?
I love leggings. They make great dance-wear.
My favourite ones are yellow and knee-length.

Viki in a nutshell
Independent / Easy-going / Extrovert

Everybody dance.

get to know

Gracie

Name: Gracie

Favourite colour: Yellow

Dancing dream: I haven't made my mind up yet, but I simply love modern dance.

Favourite dance move: The *arabesque*

Best way to spend a Saturday: Window-shopping at 'Twinkle Toes' ballet store.

I say, I say: 'I can do it perfectly!'

. . . .

PSSST! DID YOU KNOW?
Fashion's my forte. I love to look stylish.
. . . .

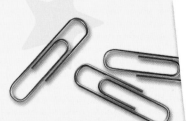

Gracie in a nutshell
Perfectionist / Competitive /
Kind-hearted

Take centre stage.

marvellous Marco

Name: Marco Quesillo

Favourite colour: Blue

Dancing dream: I'm a musician at heart so I'd love to compose the music for a big dance show.

Favourite dance move: The *pas de chat.*

Best way to spend a Saturday: Playing football then composing songs on my guitar.

I say, I say: 'I just thought of a great rhythm.'

PSSST! DID YOU KNOW?
Although I now live in Chipping Cheddar I'm originally from exotic Costa Mousa. That's where I learnt to play the conga drums!

Marco in a nutshell
Loyal / Daring /
Accident-prone

Feel the music.

hurray it's aj

Name: AJ

Favourite Colour: **Red**

Dancing Dream: **To be the trendiest boy at Camembert Academy and to perfect my headspin.**

Favourite dance move: **The hip-hop strut.**

Best way to spend a Saturday: **Skateboarding and having dance-offs with my friends.**

I say, I say: **'AJ mouse is in the house.'**

PSSST! DID YOU KNOW?
Chipping Cheddar is pretty cool, but I'm a city mouse at heart.

AJ in a nutshell
Hip / Relaxed / Fun-loving

Like my moves?

Ms. Mimi

Name: Ms. Mimi

Favourite colour: Purple

Dancing dream: To inspire a new generation of dancers.

Favourite dance move: Any move is beautiful, as long as it's danced with your heart.

Best way to spend a Saturday: I usually spend Saturday mornings marking homework, but in the afternoons I relax with a book and on Saturday evenings I often go to a dance show or recital.

I say, I say: 'Bravo, students!'

PSSST! DID YOU KNOW?
I am the headmistress at Camembert Academy but I'm also an old friend of Miss Lilly — Angelina's first ballet teacher.

Ms. Mimi in a nutshell
Encouraging / Inspiring / Warm

Life is a dance.

Let's Meet The Mouselings

Name: Polly

Favourite colour: Sky blue

Dancing dream: To be as good at ballet as Angelina.

I say, I say: 'Pretty please with cheese.'

PSSST! DID YOU KNOW?
I love putting on shows at home with Angelina.

Polly in a nutshell
Eager / Affectionate / Happy

Name: Mrs. Matilda Mouseling

Favourite colour: Maroon

I say, I say: 'Love you to bits.'

PSSST! DID YOU KNOW?
I love running up costumes for Angelina's shows

Mrs. Matilda in a nutshell
Loving / Creative / Nurturing

Name: Mr. Maurice Mouseling

Favourite colour: Brown

I say, I say: 'Just do your best.'

PSSST! DID YOU KNOW?
I'm a roving reporter for the *Mouseland Herald* newspaper so I've always got the local low-down.

Mr. Maurice in a nutshell
Entertaining / Supportive / Wise

15

Angelina's new home

"Saturday is absolutely, positively my most favourite day of the week!" cried Angelina, skipping downstairs. She pirouetted into the kitchen where her parents and little sister Polly were already eating breakfast.

BUMP! The budding ballerina tripped over a large crate. "There's not supposed to be a box there!" she said.

"Remember, Angelina? We moved yesterday and you slept in my room last night, because your room has boxes in it," Polly told her.

"Would you like to spend the day exploring outside our new home?" Dad asked.

Polly jumped up and down with excitement but Angelina shook her head. "I want to spend the day eating scones and playing with Alice just like I always do."

"Saturday can't always be the way it was," Mum said gently. "We've moved to the other side of Chipping Cheddar now."

"I know," Angelina said sadly. "Alice isn't next door and Miss Lilly isn't just around the corner anymore."

Would things ever be like they were before? Angelina imagined herself going to her old ballet class with Alice. The daydream was so vivid she could smell Miss Lilly's lavender perfume.

"Now it's all changed," she murmured. At least she could still dance – that always made her feel good.

"I need to practise my *ronds de jambes*," she told her mum. She couldn't find her stereo. "It must be in a box," she huffed. Angelina tried to practise without music but it was tricky, especially when Polly tried to join in.

"Mum says I get to do round jams too!" Polly insisted.

"It's *ronds de jambes*' and nobody's going to get to do them because I can't find my music player," said Angelina.

Mum put a CD on her player, but her music was different. "It's a new piece of music. But it has the same tempo," Mum said, counting time.

Before Angelina could try again, the CD player's batteries ran out. "I wish we'd never moved," Angelina said. "I want my own music. I don't want things to be so different."

Polly, who had been trying to copy her big sister's moves, stopped and pulled a letter from her pocket.

"I almost forgot," she said. "This came for you."

Angelina opened the letter and gulped. It was a reminder from her new school, Camembert Academy, that classes started the following week.

"Oh no," she sighed. "In this new class I might not be able to dance right." How could she make things the way they used to be?

Suddenly, she had an idea. To make Polly leave the room, Angelina told her the tooth fairy was in the kitchen. Then she grabbed the phone and dialled a number.

"Camembert Academy?" she asked, using a tea towel to muffle her voice to sound like an adult. "This is Mrs. Mouseling. We're moving back to our old house, so please give Angelina's place in your school to somebody else."

She put the phone down and looked for somewhere to hide the letter. First she put it on an armchair and covered it with her mum's tea towel. But Mrs. Mouseling came in looking for the towel and would have uncovered the letter had Mr. Mouseling not called her upstairs to take a phone call.

Angelina sighed with relief but Dad's voice made her start again – he was coming downstairs. She grabbed the letter from under the tea towel and jammed it behind a sofa cushion.

"I think I'll have a nap on the sofa," Dad called from the landing.

Angelina grabbed the letter and went to hide it in a plant pot.

"I think I should give the plants a nice watering instead," Dad said.

Angelina quickly hid the letter under a book.

"Or perhaps I'll read a book…" came Dad's voice.

Angelina grabbed the letter and darted around madly looking for a safe place to hide the envelope.

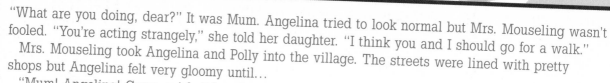

"What are you doing, dear?" It was Mum. Angelina tried to look normal but Mrs. Mouseling wasn't fooled. "You're acting strangely," she told her daughter. "I think you and I should go for a walk."

Mrs. Mouseling took Angelina and Polly into the village. The streets were lined with pretty shops but Angelina felt very gloomy until...

"Mum! Angelina! Come quick. I found something." Polly, who had run ahead, raced back to join them. She led her sister along the street and stopped in front of a fabulous ballet store. In the window was a breathtaking display of tutus, ballet slippers and tiaras.

"Ah!" gasped Angelina.

"And it's so near our new house!" said Polly.

"I suppose it is quite good," she said. Her reflection in the window made it look as if she was wearing the gorgeous yellow tutu in the display.

Back home, on the table was a beautiful vase of flowers surrounded by balloons.

Angelina hurriedly opened the lavender-coloured envelope attached – it was from Miss Lilly.

"My dear Angelina," she read. "I am writing to tell you that your new ballet teacher at Camembert is an old friend of mine. Her name is Ms. Mimi. I have told Ms. Mimi what a brilliant dancer you are and she can't wait to have you as a student."

Angelina leapt with joy. "My new teacher knows I'm a brilliant dancer! Isn't that brilliant!" she cried, hugging her mother.

"Speaking of brilliant things, Dad's been working on a surprise for you. Let's go and have a look at it!" Mum said.

She and Polly followed Mum and Dad to the attic which had been transformed into a fantastic dance studio.

Angelina could not believe her eyes. "This is all for me?" she asked. "A place to practise right in my room!"

Angelina hugged her parents and pirouetted over to the mirror with Polly copying her every move. "I love it! Thank you!" Angelina cried. "Everything's brilliant! There's a ballet shop right around the corner and my new teacher knows Miss Lilly. I can dance in my room and at my new school..."

She stopped mid-sentence and stared at her Mum and Dad. "Oh but!..."

It took the devastated little ballerina a few moments to admit exactly what she had done.

"I told a terrible lie," she said, tears welling in her eyes. "And now I won't be able to go to Camembert Academy because I phoned and..."

"...told them to give away your place because we weren't moving?" finished Mrs. Mouseling. Angelina was astonished. How did her parents know?

"Remember the phone call Dad called me upstairs for? It was Camembert," explained Mum.

"They recognise a scared little mouseling when they hear one," said Dad.

Angelina pulled the Camembert letter from behind the cushion and gave it to her father.

"I hid this, too," she said feeling ashamed.

"So you thought if we didn't know when school started, you wouldn't have to go?" Dad asked.

Angelina nodded miserably. "I think I was afraid of not being able to see Alice every Saturday and of not going to Miss Lilly's school," Angelina said. "I was trying to make everything stay the same."

Dad hugged her tightly. "Change isn't always a bad thing," he said.

"We all had to leave some things behind. But there are many exciting things here," said Mum.

"And new friends too," added Dad.

"And your old friends won't forget you," Mum promised.

Polly popped up next to Angelina holding Mum's CD player. "Dance with me, Angelina," she giggled.

"You know, Polly, I think I like this new music... it has a great tempo," Angelina said, performing several perfect *ronds de jambes* then pirouetting around the room with her sister.

"You know what? Change isn't so bad after all."

The End

Showtime SUDOKU

Hi! My friends and I are putting on a show for Ms. Mimi and we've gathered together our favourite costumes and props. We need a tutu, a wand, a pair of ballet shoes and a top hat. Can you complete this puzzle so that each of the four items appears once in every horizontal and vertical line and once in each of the four large boxes?

ANSWERS ON PAGE 77

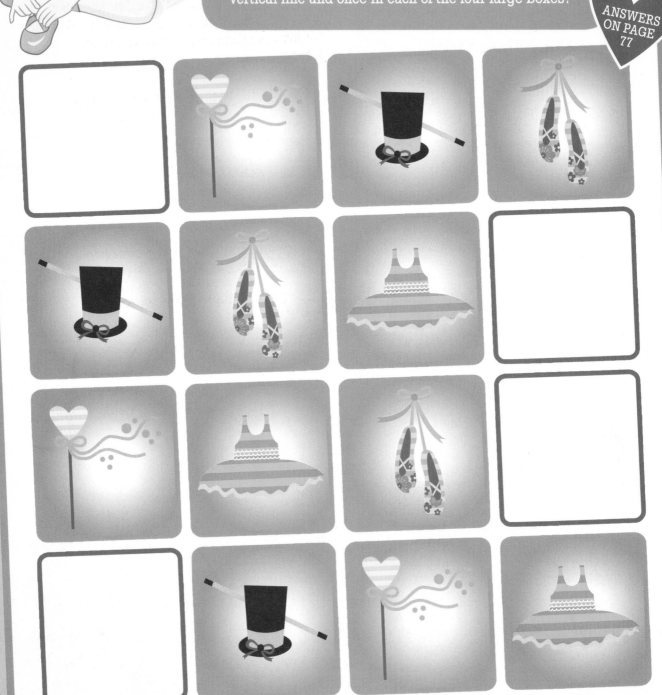

Meet and GREET

The kids at Camembert Academy have their very own school handshake which only pupils at our school know. It's a way for us to greet each other in a special way and to have fun at the same time. Why don't you invent your own greeting with friends, family or school pals?

To begin, stand facing each other and each use your right hand. If you're stuck for ideas, try incorporating some of the following moves:

- Clap palms with your friend then clap the backs of your hands together

- Hook your thumbs and waggle fingers

- Bump each other with opposite shoulders

- Pat hands on your knees and clap then repeat

- Turn with a jump so you are back to back and then wiggle

- Clasp hands high in the air and each twirl underneath

Mr. Mouseling says:

'Did you know? People around the world greet each other in different ways'

- The French kiss each other several times on alternate cheeks

- Inuit people rub noses or press their nose against the other person's forehead - this is called a 'Kunik'

- The Japanese often bow with their palms pressed together

Polly Plays School

I'm up in my amazing new attic studio playing 'ballet school' with my little sister Polly. I'm showing Polly each move but she is having trouble remembering the proper name for each position. Can you help her to learn them by matching each picture to the right word in the list opposite?

ANSWERS ON PAGE 77

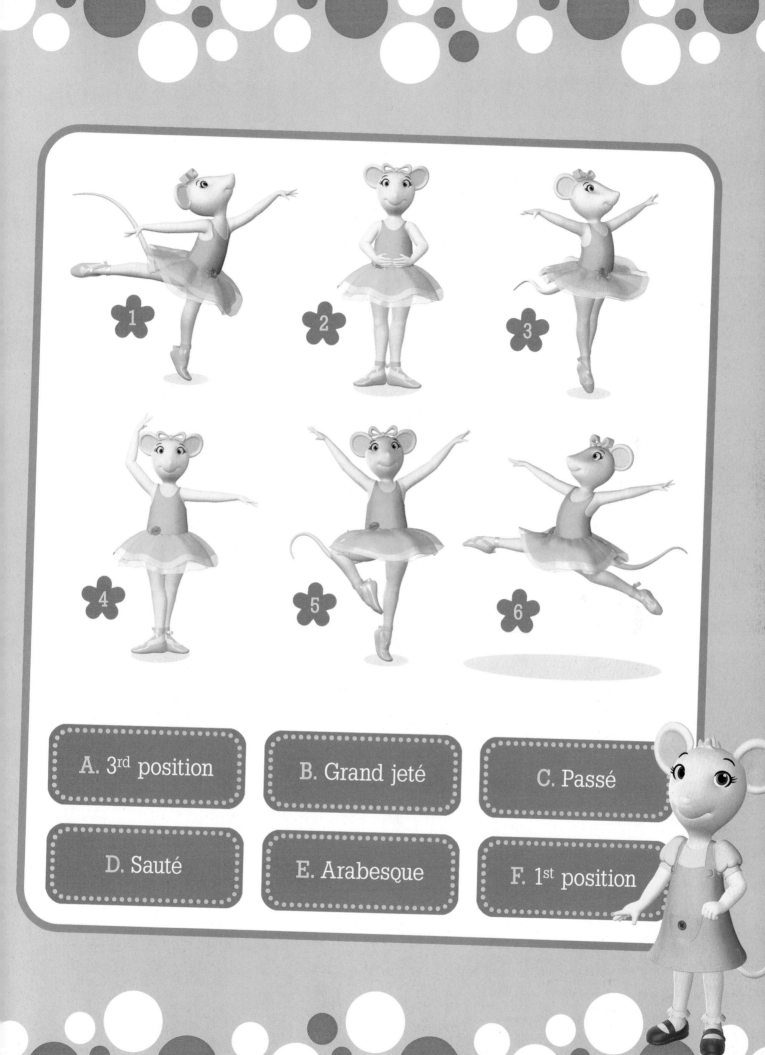

A. 3rd position

B. Grand jeté

C. Passé

D. Sauté

E. Arabesque

F. 1st position

dot-to-dot à deux

I just love to dance at every opportunity. My friends are just like me too, they simply love to practise and show off their moves. Join the dots to see how Alice, Gracie, Viki and I are dancing together.

Once you've done the dot-to-dots, grab your brightest crayons and bring these dancing friends to life!

Rhyme Time

Are you any good at riddles? Alice and I love trying to work out what these clever rhyming puzzles mean. Look at the poem below. Each line will give you a word. Write it in the empty box, then take the first letter of the word and write that in the empty box beside it. When you have all six letters, read downwards to reveal the name of one of my new school friends.

ANSWER ON PAGE 77

My first, Alice does now instead of ballet	Answer:	Letter:
My second's a Latin dance, a romantic sway	Answer:	Letter:
My third's in a hip-hop star, a friend who is sweet	Answer:	Letter:
My fourth is the thing that we mice love to eat	Answer:	Letter:
My fifth is what I skate on; it's harder than snow	Answer:	Letter:
My sixth means 'again' at the end of a show	Answer:	Letter:

My friend is:

Spot the Daddy Differences

I adore the dance studio my dad created for me in the attic of our new house. Now I can practise ballet there whenever I want. Sometimes, dad even comes up to visit me and we have a twirl together. Here's a picture of us doing just that. Can you spot and circle six differences between the top picture and the one below? Look carefully!

ANSWERS ON PAGE 77

Angelina and the hip hop kid

It was a sunny day in Chipping Cheddar and when the lunch bell sounded at Camembert Academy the doors flew open and Angelina and Gracie – one of her new friends – raced down the stone steps to find a table in the open-air Lunchtime Theatre. Another friend, Viki, had saved them a spot.

As they sat chatting and enjoying their sandwiches, a new pupil hopped up onto the stage. Angelina, Gracie and Viki gasped as he performed a funky hip-hop routine.

"That must be AJ!" said Angelina.

"I didn't know he was a hip-hop dancer," gasped Gracie.

"This is sooo exciting. I've always wanted to learn hip-hop," giggled Viki.

The girls' eyes widened as AJ beamed at them and pulled Viki up to join him on stage.

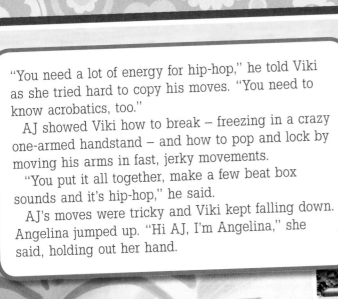

"You need a lot of energy for hip-hop," he told Viki as she tried hard to copy his moves. "You need to know acrobatics, too."

AJ showed Viki how to break – freezing in a crazy one-armed handstand – and how to pop and lock by moving his arms in fast, jerky movements.

"You put it all together, make a few beat box sounds and it's hip-hop," he said.

AJ's moves were tricky and Viki kept falling down. Angelina jumped up. "Hi AJ, I'm Angelina," she said, holding out her hand.

Instead of a normal handshake, AJ gripped her palm and showed her the coolest handshake sequence ever. "We're dancers too – ballerinas," she told him.

"I wish I could hip-hop," sighed Gracie. "I've never been able to get the hang of it."

"I can help you. You'll do great – especially since you're already ballerinas," AJ smiled.

That afternoon the girls spotted AJ hovering nervously at the door of their ballet class.

"Come on in," Gracie beckoned. "We love visitors."

"AJ's joining our ballet class," said Viki. "We have a new student, with new ideas," she told her friends.

Gracie wasn't so sure. "He's a super-good hip-hopper and he's really nice, but that doesn't mean he can do ballet," she whispered to Angelina.

Ms. Mimi called the group to the barre to practise their *pliés*. Gracie and Angelina watched as AJ added his own bouncy hip-hop flair to the knee bends.

"What do you call that?" Gracie asked. "Ballet hop?" asked Angelina. "He's got good rhythm, but that's not ballet."

"Now let's stretch our legs up, up, up and onto the barre," Ms. Mimi encouraged. AJ flipped his leg up onto the barre with ease and began bouncing his body over it.

"It must be a hip-hop warm-up!" Angelina said to Gracie as the group began *port de bras* arm positions. Then a series of rhythmic noises filled the air...

"Ballet positions to beat box sounds?" said Gracie. "That's different."

Ms. Mimi was not impressed. "Good, AJ, but a little less bouncing and please listen to the music I'm playing, and not the music you're making."

The rest of the lesson was spent practising *pas de chat*. As the bell signalled the end of the lesson, Ms. Mimi had one last announcement.

"We'll perform these steps in a *pas de deux* recital," she said. "I'll tell you who your partners are in the next class."

Angelina and Gracie glanced at each other in alarm.

When Angelina arrived home, she found her mum, and sister Polly playing musical instruments. "AJ's a really-truly good dancer, but I don't want him as my partner," she admitted. "And neither does Gracie."

Mrs. Mouseling frowned. "Why not? What's wrong with AJ?"

"We like AJ and he said he'd teach us hip-hop, but this is ballet class," she groaned. "I need a true ballerina partner for the *pas de deux*, not a hip-hop dancer, who might ruin everything."

Polly leapt up. "I'm a true ballerina! I can do a pas de doosy," she cried. Angelina laughed but still looked worried.

"Do you think maybe there isn't just one kind of ballet dancer?" Mrs. Mouseling asked.

Angelina thought hard. "Maybe not. Ballet dancers come in different shapes and sizes. And some come from different countries."

"There are xylophone-playing ballet dancers," cried Polly. "And Mouseling family ballet dancers," laughed Angelina.

Next day at school the girls discussed the coming recital. "I hope, hope, hope, with cheese on top, that AJ is my partner, he's so original!" said Viki.

"Gracie and I practise together a lot, so we're already a good pair," added Angelina, hoping Viki would get her dream partner.

Ms. Mimi had other ideas. She paired Gracie and Viki with other partners so Angelina was left with AJ.

Disappointed, Angelina drifted off into a daydream where AJ was showcasing his hip-hop moves to cheers from the audience while she stood in the shadows.

AJ took her hand. "Come on, partner," he coaxed. First they tried the *pas de chat*.

AJ went first, snapping his fingers with each step. "Not bad, but weird," Angelina said.

"It might be better if you didn't snap your fingers. Try holding your arms up like this."

AJ tried again, following Angelina's lead. This time his moves looked far more graceful.
  Ms. Mimi watched as AJ and Angelina performed two perfect *arabesques*, side by side.
  Angelina glanced at her partner, he was learning fast. "His dancing is different from mine, but it's really-truly good," she thought, looking at AJ's leg which was much higher than hers.
  "I've always wanted to get my leg up that far. How do you do it?" she asked. "Just throw it up there, Angelina," he encouraged.

After a couple of attempts, Angelina's leg position improved. "Thanks, AJ, I can't believe you just started ballet," she said.
  "Actually I started *with* ballet," he replied, performing an awesomely high *grand jeté*. "Hip-hop made me a good jumper," he explained. "I learned to push down hard on my feet. It gives you more spring."
  Following his instructions, Angelina leapt much higher in her *grand jeté*.
  The new friends enjoyed learning from each other so much that the lesson passed in a flash. Ms. Mimi was delighted. "You two are working splendidly together," she beamed.

After class Angelina ate lunch with Gracie and Viki. "I'm sorry you got AJ for a partner," Gracie said. "He is a nice mouseling, but I hope he doesn't turn your *pas de deux* into ballet-hop."

"He's not just a hip-hop dancer," Angelina told her friends. "He used to take ballet."

"You looked like you were having lots of fun," Viki said. "We were!" Angelina replied.

Just then AJ bounced onto the open-air stage and turned on the stereo. "Hip-hop, anyone?" he called. "Absolutely!" laughed Angelina, leaping up.

Viki and Gracie followed her on-stage and the foursome began performing. Angelina turned off the stereo and suggested providing a beat box soundtrack.

Within moments the new friends were freestyling. They even tried some ballet-hop, mixing ballet moves with hip-hop shapes.

"I was so wrong," thought Angelina. "I'm the luckiest ballerina in Mouseland! I have the best ballet partner and hip-hop teacher!"

The End

The Camembert CHASE

This game needs 2 – 4 players so grab your best friends and a dice.

Sometimes it's hard to get out of bed on a winter morning! But it's so important not to be late for school. My friends and I are all racing to get there on time, but who will get to the classroom first? Cut round the four pictures of Gracie, Viki, Alice and me and each choose one as your counter. If you don't want to cut the book, create your own markers. Now see if you can make it to Camembert Academy before the bell rings…

1

START HERE

2

3
Uh oh! Polly has been playing with your satchel and has taken out your pencil case. **Go back to the start.**

8

9

You've forgotten your ballet shoes. **Miss a turn.**

10

14

Your friends aren't getting along today. Choose someone to send **back to the start.**

15

Marco wants you to make up some song lyrics – make up a rhyme in 30 seconds to **move forward 4 spaces.**

16

Pick a friend to do a *pas de deux* with – pick the nearest friend ahead or behind you and share their square.

17

40

4

5

6
Ms. Mimi is walking by. Stop to say hello and **miss a go.**

7
AJ is trying to master the arabesque. Show him how and **move forward 3 spaces** if your friends approve of your moves.

11
You just love the stage! Stop to practice your moves in the Lunchbox Theatre and **miss a turn.**

12

13

18
Mrs. Mouseling's baking smells sooo scrummy! **Go back 6 spaces.**

19

20
SCHOOL TIME!

Design-a-Dance

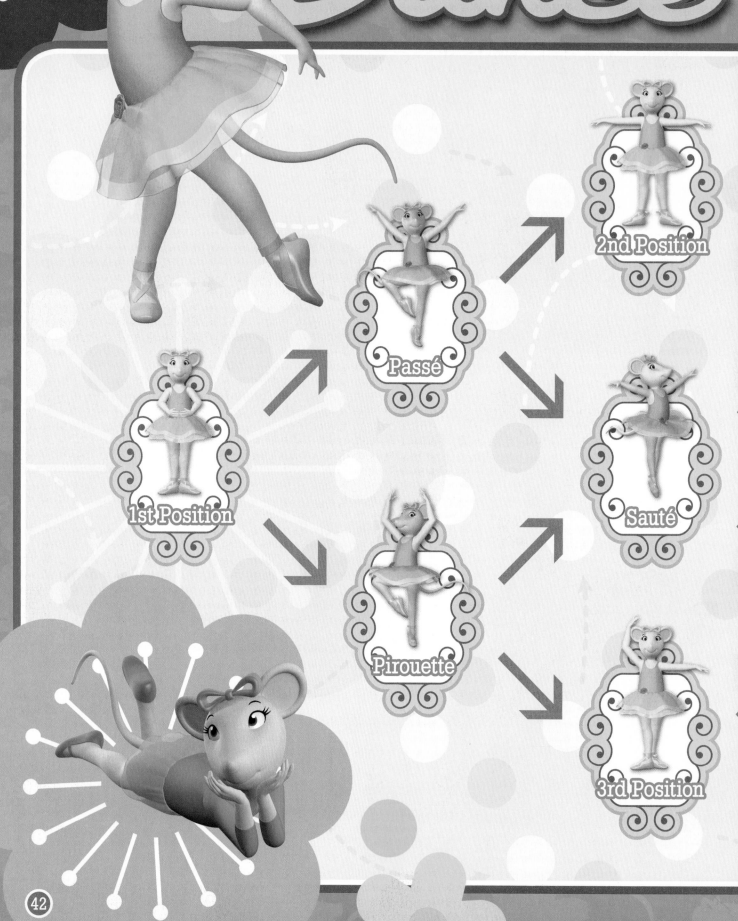

1st Position

Passé

2nd Position

Pirouette

Sauté

3rd Position

I love choreography almost as much as I love performing – choreography means deciding which moves to put together to make up the dance. You can become a brilliant choreographer with this clever 'design-a-dance' generator. Start on 1st Position and then trace your finger from left to right, choosing the moves you prefer. This will give you a sequence to practise for your very own dance recital.

Passé

Grand Jeté

Pirouette

Tendu

Arabesque

4th Position

Jeté

5th Position

Révérence

Say Cheese!

I've been busy taking photos of all the fun times I've been having since moving to my new home, but I haven't had time to write anything to remind me what each picture shows. Could you write in the captions for me so I don't forget who is pictured and what was happening at the time?

I can't believe I was worried about starting a new school. I've met such brilliant new friends like Viki and Gracie. Aren't they amazing? Now bring them to life by copying the picture on the left. Do it square by square and you'll find it easy-peasy. Don't forget to use your brightest colours for their dance clothes.

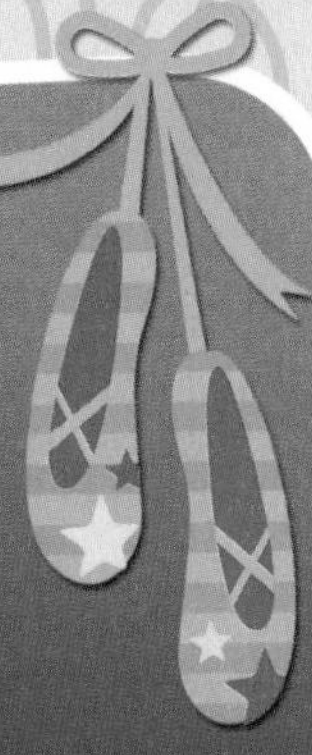

Dancing
All Over the World!

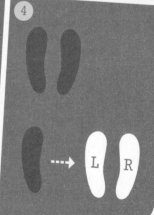

Although Angelina is passionate about ballet, she loves to perform to all kinds of music! Her favourite thing is to learn about dance styles and costumes from other faraway parts of the world. She and her friends at the Camembert Academy have clicked their fingers to Flamenco, kicked their legs to the Can-Can and even wiggled their hips in a Mouseling belly dance!

Would you like to learn some new dance steps? Here's a simple guide to three of Angelina's favourites. Each one of is from a different corner of the globe.

AUSTRIA
Waltz

The Waltz is a graceful ballroom dance, so you'll need to find a partner! To perform this step, ask a grown-up to put on an elegant tune that's not too fast, in 3:4 time. Ask your partner to be the 'leader', then hold one of their hands, putting the other round their waist. Now move backwards following the steps below.

1. Start with your feet together.

2. Take one step back with your left foot.

3. Lift up your right foot and slide it back and to the right.

4. Bring your left foot over to join your right one so that your feet are together again.

5. Now go back to step 1, but repeat the moves 1 to 4 using the opposite foot. Keep repeating the steps, alternating the feet that you use each time. This is called a Box Step.

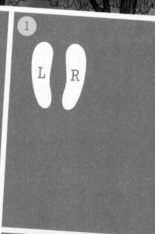

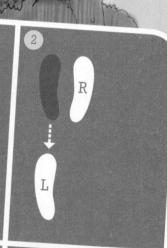

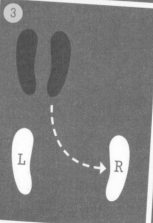

Now you're ready to whirl round and round the ballroom! Dancers should glide in an anti-clockwise direction.

USA
Line-dancing

Cowboys and cowgirls love standing in rows then rocking out to their favourite country and western songs! Find some friends who would like to try line-dancing, then give these steps a try. When you are line-dancing at a party or concert a caller will shout out, 'Take it to the left!' every time they want you to do this move.

1. Start with your feet together.

2. Step to the side with your left foot.

3. Now bring your right foot across your left.

4. Step to the side with your left foot.

5. Now bring your right foot in to touch your left. When it's time to 'take it back now!' just take three steps back and touch your feet together again.

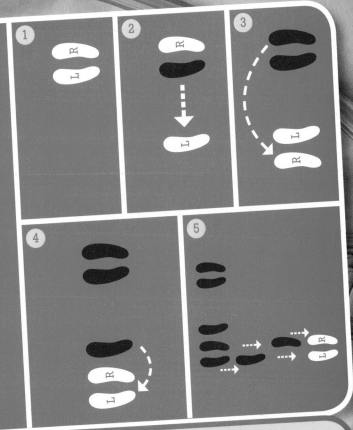

Once you've got this basic line dance sequence, you can add all kinds of extra moves on top! Try hopping forward and back, doing a box square or clapping your hands.

CUBA
Salsa

Salsa is a fun and vibrant dance created by Spanish-speaking people from the Caribbean – it's a real fusion of styles! You can bop to Salsa on your own, with a partner, or in a group of friends. The important thing is to feel the rhythm and really move your hips with each step.

1. Start with your feet together.

2. Step forwards with your left foot and shimmy on the spot.

3. Now bring your left foot back to your right and shimmy to the beat.

4. Step backwards with your right foot and shimmy on the spot.

5. Bring your right foot forward to meet your left again and shimmy to the beat.

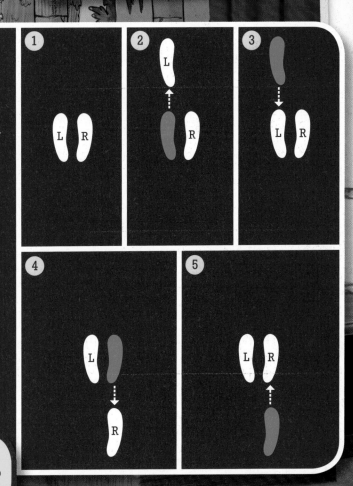

Just think of it as a step forwards and a step back with a pause between. Ask a grown-up to put on some upbeat Latin music, then Salsa!

Make it!

Gracie's
Glitter Glue Stars

Gracie loves to be the star of the show – just like me. With her craft idea for these gorgeous glittery decorations, you can't fail to shine. These pretty stars are great for sticking on windows or hanging on the tree over the festive season.

You'll need:

Glitter in any colour you like – we love gold and silver!

Plastic food wrap

A large piece of cardboard

PVA glue

String for hanging, optional

PLEASE ASK AN ADULT FOR HELP WHEN USING SCISSORS

Instructions

1
Secure the plastic food wrap with tape onto the cardboard, pulling it smooth and taut.

2
Make star shapes on the plastic wrap with the glue. Fill in the centre of the shapes with glue as well.

3 If you want to be able to hang your stars up, attach a loop of string to the top of each by putting the ends into the wet glue.

4 Sprinkle the glue stars with glitter so that they are completely covered.

5 Leave the glue to dry for 48 hours.

6 Untape the plastic wrap from the cardboard, then gently peel the plastic away from the glittery star, working in from each point. Use scissors if necessary.

7 You will be left with beautiful sparkly star decorations to brighten any room.

Angelina's gift for Ms. Mimi

The Mouseling home was a hive of activity. Mrs. Mouseling was baking muffins and Polly was playing at being a schoolgirl, like her big sister.

"Look, Mum, I'm Angelina and this is my pretend satchel," Polly squeaked as she ran around putting things in a brown paper bag.

"Ding Dong!" Polly ran to answer the door. Viki, Gracie and Marco stood on the doorstep.

"What's all the excitement about?" Dad asked.

"It's Ms. Mimi's birthday," Angelina told him, as the friends gathered on the sofa. Viki had her piggy bank, Gracie had her purse, Marco had brought his guitar and Angelina was writing a list.

"Ms. Mimi's at school marking homework on Saturdays, isn't she?" Dad asked.

"Until one o'clock. Then she walks right past the Lunchtime Theatre. That's where the surprise will be," Angelina smiled.

"I made a list of what we need for the party," Angelina said. "If we put all our money together we can buy something really, really nice," Viki said, shaking her piggy bank.

"Is it OK if I stay here while you go shopping?" Marco asked. "I'm composing."

"Pom-cosing?" Polly asked. Marco laughed and explained that composing meant creating a song.

"I still need to write the lyrics," he said. Polly was confused. "Lyri..ri..rricks?"

"Lyrics are the words to a song. Like icing on a cake," said Angelina.

"Speaking of cakes, did you put 'birthday cake' on the list?" asked Gracie.

"Of course. Mum said she'll bake one," Angelina replied. The girls jumped up and down in excitement.

Angelina, Gracie and Viki stopped at 'Twinkle Toes' ballet shop. In the window was a stunning pair of silver ballet slippers.

"Oh, they're sooo amazing," cooed Viki. "Ms. Mimi's going to love them!" nodded Gracie.

Gracie and Viki went inside but Angelina slipped into one of her daydreams. She could see Ms. Mimi unwrapping the slippers and thanking her for the wonderful gift.

Gracie's voice interrupted the vision. "Angelina, the lady in 'Twinkle Toes' said the slippers are made of satin and somebody sewed them by hand... but we don't have enough money."

"But we need to get Ms. Mimi a great present, to show her how much we love her!" said Angelina sadly.

What could they do? Viki had a great idea. "Those ballet slippers were made by hand," she gasped.

"And all of us have hands!" smiled Angelina. "Mum has satin in her sewing basket. We can make the slippers ourselves!"

Back home, the friends got busy snipping and sewing scraps of fabric and ribbons. They stood back to admire their work. But, oh dear...!

"Hmm, maybe we should make a tutu instead?" said Gracie, looking down at the tatty-looking shoes. Before the others could answer, Mr. Mouseling called up to let them know Mrs. Mouseling had finished the cake. They rushed downstairs to find a rose-covered cake topped with a single candle.

"It's pretty but I think it needs to be bigger," said Gracie. Marco and Angelina agreed and Angelina began pulling pans out of the cupboards. Soon she, Viki and Polly were ramming dozens of Mrs. Mouseling's muffins into the tins and topping them with heaps of icing.

Meanwhile Gracie and Marco were busy making a tutu, but they were in such a hurry that they were not at all careful and accidentally cut the toe off one of their home-made slippers.

55

Later, the friends got together in the kitchen to show each other their work.

"What happened to the cake?" Gracie asked, staring at Angelina and Viki's lopsided disaster.

"What happened to the slipper?" Angelina asked, looking at the ruined slipper. "We cut it by mistake," said Marco.

The tutu had come out even worse!

The kitchen clock struck midday. "Oh! We have to leave for the party in ten minutes," cried Gracie.

The friends tried frantically to fix the cake. Marco whistled his song as they worked. Angelina began to make up lyrics.

"We love you, yes we do. Oh we love you," she sang. Her heart sank as she remembered all they still had to do.

Angelina and Gracie rushed off to decorate the stage at the Lunchbox Theatre. They had hoped to find some balloons in the school but there were none so they had to string up daisies instead.

"I think we did a pretty good job," said Gracie. "Ms. Mimi does like flowers," nodded Angelina.

Marco, Viki and Polly arrived. "I ran out of fabric to fix the slipper," Viki said. At least they still had the enormous cake.

Marco carried it carefully towards the stage, then Polly picked a dandelion and blew on the seeds.

A gust of wind caught them and sent them under Marco's nose. "AAAAAAAAtttishooooooo!" he sneezed.

He dropped the cake and it smashed into pieces on the ground. Another gust of wind scattered the daisy banner in a dozen different directions, leaving the stage bare.

The friends were heartbroken. "No gift. No decorations. No cake…" sniffed Angelina, wiping away a tear.

All seemed lost until Polly came to the rescue. "We could use my muffin as a cake!" she said, pulling one out of her pretend satchel.

"Thanks, Polly! What else is in that bag?" asked Angelina. The little mouseling pulled drawing paper and crayons out and the friends got busy.

Within minutes they'd made a beautiful card for Ms. Mimi, put a candle in the muffin and decorated the table with a ring of daisies.

At that very moment the birthday girl arrived. "Isn't that beautiful?" smiled Ms. Mimi, looking at the table. "Is someone having a party?"

"Surprise!" yelled Angelina, Gracie, Viki, Marco and Polly. "It's a birthday party for you," said Angelina.

Ms. Mimi gasped in delight as Gracie handed her the card.

"We drew it ourselves," said Viki.

"And here's your cake. Sort of," added Polly.

"There aren't any real presents. It all went wrong…" said Gracie sadly.

But then Angelina piped up. "Wait a minute! We couldn't buy you anything, but we do have something for you," she said.

She whispered to her friends and Marco picked up his guitar. Together, they sang:

'Just one thing that we want to say, We love you! Yes, we do! Oh we love you!'

"That song is the most wonderful gift in the world," Ms. Mimi said when they'd finished. Everyone looked confused.

"Gifts don't have to be things you buy at a shop," Ms. Mimi explained. "To be really good, all a gift needs is to have lots of love in it."

Hugging Angelina and her friends, Ms. Mimi bit into her birthday muffin and sat down to listen again to her surprise birthday song.

The End

Story search

1. How many cups are hanging on the wall?

2. What is on the shelf next to the candlestick?

3. What colour are the oven-gloves hanging on the chimney breast?

& find!

If you've read the story you'll know that my friends and I worked really hard to make Ms. Mimi's birthday special. So let's see if you can work just as hard spotting details. Take a look at this picture and try to answer the questions.

ANSWERS ON PAGE 77

8. Can you draw your own birthday surprise for Ms. Mimi in the space on the table?

7. How many yellow notes are stuck on the side of the pink cupboard?

6. Which piece of kitchen equipment is next to the blue pot on the stove?

4. What are we looking at on the table?

5. Which room are we in?

design a tutu

Tutus are so cute. Wearing the delicate tulle skirts is absolutely positively one of the best things about ballet. Can you design me a costume for my next show? I'll need a pretty leotard and tutu. Remember, I adore pink, but I also love bright and pastel colours, shiny jewels and sparkles. Make me look fantastic.

Putting on a show!

A perfect performance is all about the details.
Here are my Top Ten things to think about when planning your show.

1. The Right Role

Not everyone is a born performer but you can still take part. A successful show is all about teamwork. You might want to work on costumes, helping the dancers dress; or on props, collecting the objects to be used on stage and handing them out at the right moment. You could be a stage manager and ensure everything runs smoothly or be in the box office handing out tickets. There's a fun job for everyone.

2. Think up a Theme

All the best shows have a theme or story. You could base yours on a famous fairy tale or simply something you love like 'animals' or 'toys' or 'sport'.

3. Set the Stage

You may not have a stage, but you can certainly prepare the area you'll perform in. Make sure any furniture is cleared away so you have plenty of room to dance without tripping over.

4. Lovely Lighting

To set the mood, close the curtains, turn out the lights and give your backstage crew as many torches as you can find. When you're ready to perform, they can use them to create spotlights or whirl them around during faster dance numbers.

5. Clever Costumes

Raid your dressing-up box and your wardrobe for great outfits. Will you be a swan, a fairy or a witch?

6. Proper Props

These are the objects the performers might carry on stage. They could be things like a hat, a wand, a broomstick, a teapot. Make sure you have these ready and waiting before the show starts.

7. Programme

Your audience will want to read all about your show, so use plain paper and pens or pencils to make a perfect programme. You might like to write a bit about the story and also list the people who will be in it and which parts they play.

8. Tickets, Please

You'll need tickets too! Create your own and include the name of the show, the date, time and place where it will take place. Give them to anyone you want to invite.

9. Refreshments

The audience will need refreshment during the 'interval' – the break between the acts – or after the show. Get some water or fruit squash ready.

10. Brilliant Bouquets

The leading dancers are always presented with flowers when they take their bows. Make posies of dandelions or daisies – ask your parents before you pick anything from the garden. If you can't find real flowers, make your own, using tissue paper scrunched up and taped to pipecleaners.

Viki's Dance Directory

Viki is always trying out new styles of dance. She knows so many, I just can't keep up. Can you help me sort out the jumbled-up words below to reveal eight different dances I could try...

ANSWERS ON PAGE 77

1. Gonta — Answer:

2. Alsas — Answer:

3. Barmu — Answer:

4. Baams — Answer:

5. Plyhi-Nod — Answer:

6. Hac-ach — Answer:

7. Lenin Candig — Answer:

8. Linen lagbycd — Answer:

marco's Musical Mayhem

My clever friend Marco can play almost any instrument he picks up. Listed below are just a few! Can you find them hidden in the grid? They can run sideways, up, down or diagonally.

ANSWERS ON PAGE 77

- Clarinet
- Double Bass
- Drums
- Flute
- Guitar
- Harp
- Piano
- Saxophone
- Tambourine
- Triangle
- Trombone
- Violin

R	A	T	I	U	G	Q	F	L	Y	T	S
O	C	K	B	P	A	P	E	B	M	L	T
O	V	Y	J	F	G	I	L	S	V	J	A
F	L	U	T	E	C	A	G	E	T	P	M
A	E	P	R	E	K	N	N	P	E	U	B
R	D	K	O	G	S	O	A	A	N	X	O
E	N	Y	M	V	H	R	I	V	I	F	U
D	A	T	B	P	A	N	R	N	R	C	R
R	G	N	O	H	R	E	T	B	A	T	I
U	P	X	N	A	P	V	I	O	L	I	N
M	A	C	E	R	F	L	L	Y	C	K	E
S	S	A	B	E	L	B	U	O	D	P	A

65

Matilda Mouseling's Chilly Snowballs

Polly and I love cooking with our mum. This is our favourite recipe to make at Christmas because the choccy snowballs are sooooo amazing and yummy. It's especially brilliant because you don't need to use the oven at all – you just put them into the fridge to chill.

To make 40 snowballs you will need:
12 oz (340 g) white chocolate chips
4 tablespoons double cream
2 extra tablespoons double cream
6 oz (170 g) finely ground almonds
1 pack of sweetened flaked coconut

What to do:
1. Place the chocolate chips and 4 tablespoons of cream in a medium bowl and then melt them by placing the bowl over a pan of hot water (not boiling). Stir until smooth.

2. Stir in the extra 2 tablespoons of cream and the almonds.

3. Spread the mixture in a lightly greased baking pan.

4. Put in the fridge for about one hour, until firm.

5. Take the mixture out of the fridge and cut into 1.25 in x 1.25 in (3 x 3 cm) squares.

6. Roll each square into a ball.

7. Pour your coconut flakes onto a plate and then roll each ball in the flakes and place on a plate.

8. Chill and serve.

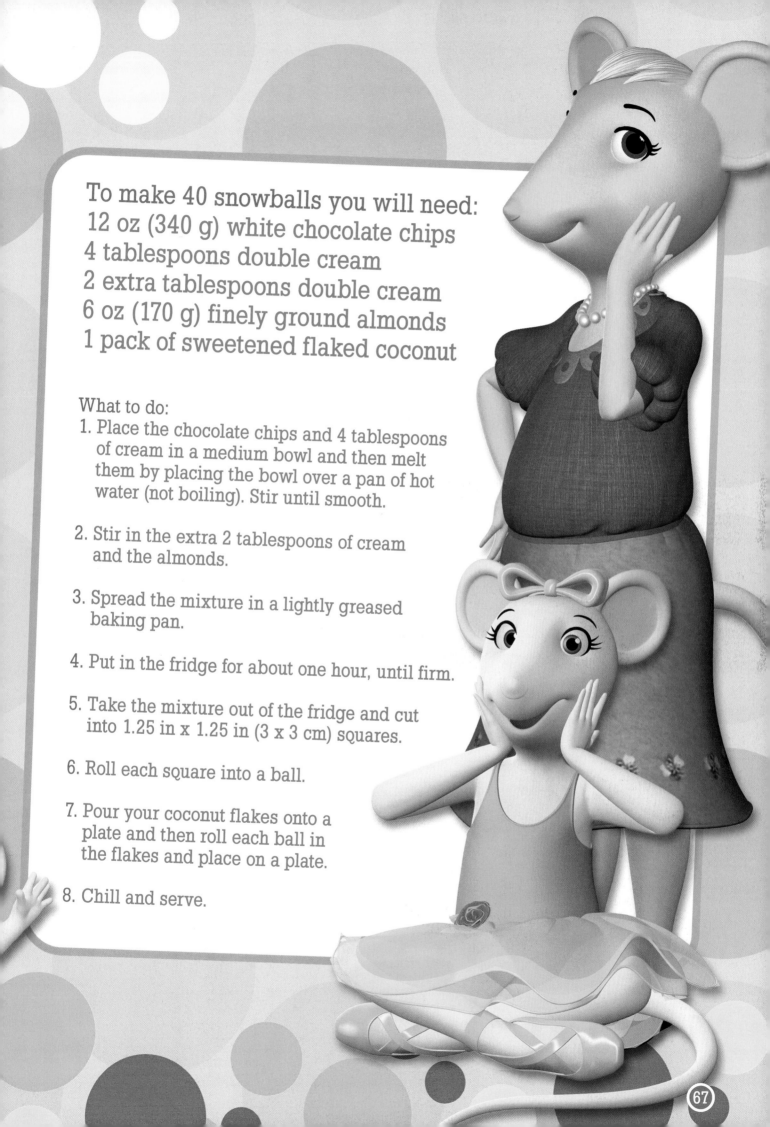

Angelina's Crazy Solo

One morning in the Camembert Academy dance studio, Ms. Mimi gathered her students together.

Angelina and her friends gazed in excitement at the large top hat Ms. Mimi was wearing.

"I love surprises," said Angelina. "Is it a magic trick?" Marco asked.

Ms. Mimi shook her head. "We're going to plan and put on our very own show."

Everyone twirled around the studio with excitement.

"I love shows!" laughed Angelina. Ms. Mimi took off the hat, turned it upside down and emptied lots of scraps of paper into it.

"What are those?" Alice asked. "The names of all the different things that go into making a dance performance," Ms. Mimi explained.

Ms. Mimi led the class to the open-air theatre. "It takes teamwork to dance together and teamwork to put on a show," she said.

Alice grabbed hold of Angelina's hand. "This is fun!" she squealed.

Ms. Mimi asked her pupils to reach into the hat one by one to pick out their job for the show.

"I want to be a dancer," cried Angelina. "Me too," said Gracie. Viki went first. "Choreographer," she read from her scrap of paper. "Super! I get to make up the steps of our dance!"

Marco was next. He would design the stage. Alice was confused by her pick. "Stage manager? What's that?" she asked.

"It's the person who makes sure everyone works together," Marco explained. "So the whole show will turn out perfectly," added Angelina.

So far everyone had been pleased with their roles. Angelina and Gracie were both itching to be dancers but Ms. Mimi warned that there would only be one in this show.

The anxious friends closed their eyes and reached into the hat. Gracie read her paper first. "Props. Oh!" she exclaimed. "I suppose that means you picked 'dancer', Angelina."

"No, I picked 'soloist'," Angelina replied. Suddenly, she remembered the meaning of the word. "Soloist means one dancer, dancing all by herself on stage! Right, Ms. Mimi?" she cried, jumping up and down happily.

Ms. Mimi nodded but, seeing that Gracie was disappointed the kind teacher explained how Gracie was perfect for props and costume mistress as she had an eye for fashion and style.

Angelina rushed over and high-fived Gracie, who felt much better now.

Back home, Angelina excitedly told her family about her part in the show.
They were busy working on a quilt for Angelina's bed. Mr. Mouseling was cutting cloth into squares, Polly was putting the squares into piles and Mrs. Mouseling was sewing them onto the quilt.
"I will be the only one dancing on stage, like a star ballerina!" Angelina said. "It's nice your class is working together," said Mrs. Mouseling.

Polly asked Angelina to help with the new quilt but Angelina had other things on her mind.
"I have to go and practise my solo," she said, running upstairs.
"A solo... I think it should be about... stars!" she thought.

As usual, she slipped easily into a daydream and imagined Ms. Mimi presenting her with a beautiful star. "Thank you, Ms. Mimi, it's such fun being a star!" she cried, twirling through the sky.

BUMP! Angelina had been so busy twirling she hadn't noticed Polly come upstairs and ran into her.

"Look! Mum cut out a pink star for your dancing-by-yourself solo," Polly said, offering Angelina a star-shaped piece of quilt material.

"That's just what I was dreaming about," smiled Angelina.

Next day, at first rehearsal, everyone was raring to go and Angelina couldn't wait to show her friends the quilt star and explain her idea. But before she could utter a word, Viki began talking.

"I choreographed a dance about a super-fun Spring fairy in the forest who uses her magic wand to open up all the petals of the flowers."

Marco, Gracie and Alice loved the theme. Gracie went straight off to design flower-shaped props and Marco immediately began his forest set design.

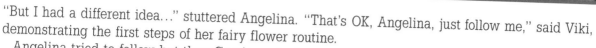

"But I had a different idea…" stuttered Angelina. "That's OK, Angelina, just follow me," said Viki, demonstrating the first steps of her fairy flower routine.

Angelina tried to follow but then Gracie rushed over to give her an enormous yellow flower.

"How can I dance holding this?" Angelina asked, bumping into lunch tables as she struggled with the heavy prop.

Things got worse when Marco finished his set. "See, it's a forest," he explained.

There were so many trees that Angelina had barely room to move. She ran across the stage to attempt a *jeté* but bumped straight into a tree with her huge flower.

The tree fell down. Marco hauled it upright and Angelina tried again with a smaller leap but she fell on top of her flower and sent all the trees crashing down like dominoes.

"My props!" said Gracie "My set!" cried Marco. "My dance!" shouted Viki, while Alice put her head in her hands.

"I thought a solo was going to be fun," Angelina groaned. "This is no fun at all."

That evening, Angelina sat with her family working on the quilt but even the sight of the beautiful bedding couldn't stop her worrying about her solo.

"There are too many trees, Gracie's flower is too big and Viki doesn't want to hear any of my ideas," she told her parents.

"I'm sorry, Angelina," said Dad.

"Maybe if you talk to each other, it will all work out," said Mum.

Angelina didn't see how it could work out when the show was the next day.

"Look, we're all done," smiled Polly. She showed her big sister the quilt featuring a big pink star. "We're a quilting team," she said. "And at least we listened to you, Angelina – see there's a pink star right in the middle of your quilt."

"Thanks, Polly," said Angelina, trying to muster a smile. "I wish being a solo star at school was as much fun as this... maybe I should tell Ms. Mimi I don't want to dance the solo."

The next morning at school she went to tell Ms. Mimi she wanted to pull out of the show, but before she could speak, Gracie rushed over. "I saw yesterday that the flower was too big. I made the star you brought into a fairy wand instead," she told Angelina.

Angelina was too happy for words. Then Marco told her he'd decided one tree on stage would give her more room to perform.

"Now, I can really turn and leap. Thank you, Marco!" she cried.

"Places for the show, please!" Alice-the-stage-manager called. Angelina turned to Ms. Mimi.

"All I wanted to say is that everyone worked so hard and I love working as a team!" she said before racing off to the stage.

Angelina had decided other things were more important than taking the limelight. When the show began, Ms. Mimi was delighted to see Angelina invite Viki and Gracie to dance with her. Then Alice and Marco joined them on stage.

"Dancing a solo is wonderful," Angelina thought as they took their bows. "But working as a team and dancing together – that's even more stupendous!"

The End

What Winter Means to Me...

This is really-truly one of my favourite times of year. Crisp, frosty mornings on the way to school, cosy evenings spent at home with my family. I love it. Here are all the things that make winter such a wonderful season.

Hot chocolate with marshmallows on top / Ice skating / Snowball fights with AJ and Marco / Mittens on strings and warm woolly scarves / Putting on a Christmas dance show / Wrapping up warm and going for long walks / Snuggling on the sofa with Polly / Carol singing in Chipping Cheddar / Our crackling log fire / Holly berries and ivy leaves / Finding the perfect pink wrapping paper / Blowing dragon smoke puffs with your breath / Frosty footprints on the pavement

What does winter mean to you?

....

....

....

....

....

....

....

....

....

....

....

....

....

....